This
Treasure Cove Story
belongs to

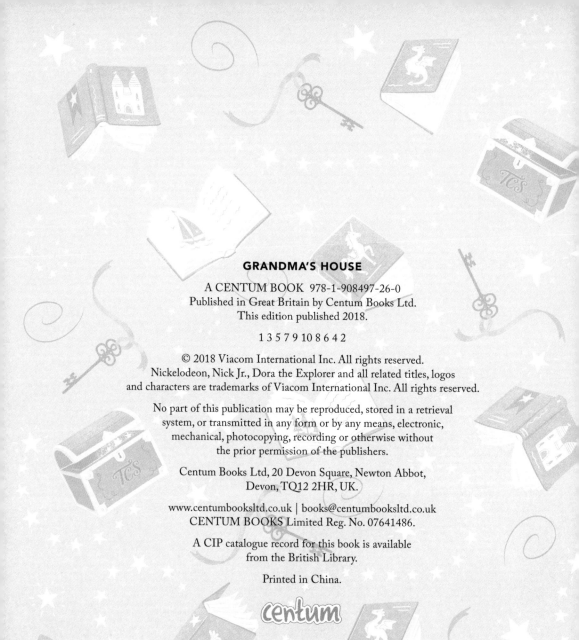

GRANDMA'S HOUSE

A CENTUM BOOK 978-1-908497-26-0
Published in Great Britain by Centum Books Ltd.
This edition published 2018.

1 3 5 7 9 10 8 6 4 2

Centum Books Ltd, 20 Devon Square, Newton Abbot,
Devon, TQ12 2HR, UK.

www.centumbooksltd.co.uk | books@centumbooksltd.co.uk
CENTUM BOOKS Limited Reg. No. 07641486.

A CIP catalogue record for this book is available
from the British Library.

Printed in China.

centum

nickelodeon

A Treasure Cove Story

Grandma's House

By Courtney Carbone
Based on an episode by Eric Weiner
Illustrated by Dan Haskett and Brenda Goddard

Dora loves her grandma, Abuela, very much.
   So when Dora heard that Abuela had a cold,
Dora and Mami put together a basket of very
special treats to take to her.
   When the basket was ready, Dora and Boots
left for Abuela's house.
   '*¡Cuidado!*' Mami reminded them. 'Don't let
Swiper swipe the basket!'

Dora and Boots set off into the forest. They couldn't wait to get to Abuela's house with the basket of treats.

'But Dora, how do we get to Abuela's house?' Boots asked.

'Let's ask Map,' Dora said.

Map knew the way to go! He showed Dora and Boots that they would need to go over the Bumpy Bridge and across Turtle River to get to grandma's house.

Dora and Boots had to travel through the forest to get to the Bumpy Bridge. The forest was very quiet – except for a small rustling sound. Dora looked at Boots. 'Did you hear that?' she asked. 'It sounds like Swiper the Fox!'

It *was* Swiper! He jumped out of the bushes and reached for the basket.

Dora and Boots said, 'Swiper, no swiping!'

Swiper snapped his fingers and said, 'Oh, mannn!' Then he ran away without the basket. The two friends continued on their journey to Abuela's house.

Soon Dora and Boots arrived at the Bumpy Bridge. They had to be very careful crossing it.

'Wow!' said Dora. 'This bridge sure is bouncy!'

Boots held on to the basket tightly, but the bridge was just too shaky! He accidentally dropped the basket into the valley below. 'The basket! The basket!' Boots cried.

'Don't worry,' Dora told him. 'We'll get the basket back.' She checked inside Backpack for something they could use to get the basket.
   'A fishing rod!' she exclaimed. 'This will work.'

Dora carefully lowered the line
and hooked it onto the basket handle.
She gently lifted the basket back up.
'We got it!' Boots exclaimed.

Dora and Boots entered a forest blossoming with colourful flowers and green leaves. Long vines hung from the trees. One of the vines was moving.

Suddenly, Swiper swung out of the tree and tried to swipe Abuela's basket!

'Duck!' Dora warned Boots.
They both ducked down so that Swiper could not reach them. Swiper swung past – into a nearby tree! The friends had kept the basket away from the sneaky fox once again.

Dora and Boots still had to find Turtle River,
but they also needed a rest! They set the
basket down on a rock for a moment. Suddenly,
the basket started to move. The rock was
actually a turtle!

Dora and Boots followed the turtle. It led them right to Turtle River! They were very happy, but there was a problem.

'How will we get across Turtle River?' Boots asked.

Dora knew she and Boots
could ask for help. They could
get across the river on the backs
of five turtles!

Dora and Boots counted each turtle. *'Una. Dos. Tres. Cuatro. Cinco.'* One by one, the turtles swam into a line and the two friends carefully hopped from shell to shell. Soon Dora and Boots were safely on the other side of Turtle River.

Dora and Boots had almost reached Abuela's house when they met a talking tree.

'Bring the basket a little closer,' the tree said. 'I just want to take a sniff.'

'Careful, Boots. I don't think that's a normal tree,' Dora warned.

'It's Swiper the Fox!' Boots cried. That sneaky fox still wanted Abuela's treats, but Dora and Boots stopped him again by saying, 'Swiper, no swiping!'

Finally, Dora and Boots arrived at
grandma's house. They were proud to
have safely made it over the Bumpy Bridge,
across Turtle River and past Swiper the Fox.
   'Abuela!' Dora and Boots called. Abuela
invited them inside.

Abuela gave Dora and Boots big kisses. She was very happy that they had come to visit her! 'How are you feeling, Abuela?' Dora asked. 'Fine, Dora. I just have a little cold,' Abuela said.

Dora gave the basket of treats to Abuela.
Inside were yummy cookies, fresh mangoes
and delicious *arroz con leche*.

There was also a special surprise. Dora
had drawn a picture for Abuela.

'Dora and Boots, I love all my treats,' said
Abuela. 'Thanks to you, I'm feeling better
already! *¡Gracias!*'

Dora and Boots were happy that
Abuela liked the basket of treats.
'¡Lo hicimos!' Dora said.
'We did it!' shouted Boots.

Going to grandma's house had been
a wonderful adventure and seeing her
smile was the best part of all.

Treasure Cove Stories

Book list may be subject to change.